# BLIND CURVE

TURBO

ARGED

# BLIND CURVE

## ACURA INTEGRA

Elizabeth Karre

MINNEAPOLIS

Darby Creek
A division of Lerner Publishing Group, Inc.
241 First Avenue North
Minneapolis, MN 55401 U.S.A.

Website address: www.lernerbooks.com

The images in this book are used with the permisison of:
Cover and interior photograph © Transtock/SuperStock.

Main body text set in Janson Text LT Std 12/17.
Typeface provided by Linotype AG.

The Cataloging-in-Publication Data for *Blind Curve* is on file at the Library of Congress.
ISBN: 978–1–4677–1244–6 (LB)
ISBN: 978–1–4677–1666–6 (EB)

Manufactured in the United States of America
1 – BP – 7/15/13

# CHAPTER ONE

"What's going on?" I yell. No one answers.

I stand on tiptoe to see over the heads of all the kids pushing and talking right outside the school doors. I'm a short girl. I can't see anything except flashing red and blue lights.

A loud siren makes me jump. An ambulance speeds off down Lexington.

I tap a girl in front of me.

"What happened?"

She looks worried. "Someone got hurt."

Before I can ask more, my phone buzzes. It's Pakou.

*Bad news. Come bus stop.*

I see her waiting as I run across the street, barely looking for cars.

*Watch out!* she yells in Hmong. She looks sick.

"What? What?" I say.

She grabs my arm. "You didn't even look—you could get hit." She starts to cry. "I saw it, I saw it all. They came flying down the street, racing. Kids were messing around. Somebody got pushed into the street and he got hit, hit by one of the racers. But they didn't stop. I couldn't even call 911, I was so scared. And the ambulance was here so fast. But he must be hurt so bad. Or . . ."

I give her a hug. She's shaking.

"But, Penny, that's not the bad news," she says, wiping away tears. "The bad part is that one of the cars looked just like yours."

# CHAPTER TWO

I don't own a car. I take the bus to school, or my brothers might drive me if they're feeling nice. I take the city bus when I go other places if my parents won't give me a ride. I don't even have a license yet. I'm seventeen, but nobody in my family thinks it's worth the money and hassle for me to take driver's ed. It's easier to get a license when you're eighteen.

But I do drive sometimes, and I do have a car. A 1999 Acura Integra. I just don't own it. Yet.

The car's in my brother Bee's name. I

found it online, and he took me to see it. He paid for it and signed the papers. But we both know it's mine. I'm paying for it by doing his homework.

The Teg's a garage queen right now. She wasn't in good shape when we got her, and there's a lot I want to mod. And it takes me a while to get money for each part we buy.

Part of me wishes that she'd never be finished. The time Bee and I spend working on her is the best. But he's determined to have her ready for my eighteenth birthday. And I know no car is ever truly finished. But I just have a feeling that our time together will be over once he says the car is done.

We do take the Teg out sometimes. That's when I drive. Bee and my oldest brother, Toua, even made a video one time of me driving up and down our street, testing the exhaust. They're laughing and yelling, "Penny breakin' the law, breakin' the law!" so loud you can hardly hear the car. Then they posted it on YouTube.

If my parents ever found out, I'd be dead.

But there are a lot of things my parents don't know about their kids. Anyway, the Integra mostly stays in the garage.

When I get home, I go straight to the garage. The Teg's there, next to my mom's minivan. The hood is open and the work light is hanging over it.

I put my hand on the engine. It's sparkling clean, like always. It feels warm. From driving? From the work light? I feel dizzy. My brain shuts down.

No way was my brother Bee one of the racers. If he was driving the Teg, it was just to test something. He has study hall last period and he leaves school early lots. My mom doesn't like it, but sometimes one of my sisters has to drop her kids off before my mom gets home from work. And Bee swears to her that he just comes home and does his homework here instead of in study hall. Really, he leaves his homework in the Teg for me to do, and he works on his car or my car.

I see his schoolbooks on the seat now. I open the door to the house and yell to my mom, “I’m home!” I close the door and settle in the Teg to do our homework.

I’m jumpy, waiting for Bee to come out and join me. But he doesn’t.

# CHAPTER THREE

I do English first, trying to lose myself in reading. I skim Bee's American History and answer the essay questions. (Are you wondering about our handwriting? It's pretty similar.)

But while I'm working on my math, my mind wanders. It's not like we think we're too good for street racing. Bee and Toua and their friends go to the spots around the warehouses on University where people hang out with their cars and sometimes race at night. They've even taken me a couple of times so I could get some ideas for the Teg. (Again, my parents would kill me if they knew.)

But they've never raced their cars there . . . at least that I know. Even if they did, racing around some warehouses and side streets when there's no one around except other gearheads is different than speeding down a crowded busy street by a school in the afternoon. Racing in Midway pisses off the cops, but racing on Lexington? That's just stupid. And wrong.

Besides, my brothers keep pretty clean. Sure, they like to act tough with their friends and at school and they love to show off their cars, but they don't get in trouble. They don't have anything to do with the Hmong gangs.

Once my family was having a picnic at Como, and Johnny Xiong was there playing flag football. He's in my grade and he waved to me.

"How do you know Johnny?" Toua demanded.

"He's in my health class," I said.

"Why is he waving to you?"

"I don't know. What's your problem?"

Then my parents butted in, and Toua told them that Johnny and his brother had just joined a gang. My parents forbid me to have anything to do with him or anyone else who was a disgrace to the Hmong people. Then my dad and uncles started talking about the Vietnam War, and that's when I stopped listening. Nobody asked how Toua knew who was in a gang or not.

# CHAPTER FOUR

While my thoughts are spinning, my niece comes to the door and says my mom needs me inside.

If your parents are immigrants and you're a girl, you know what it's like. My parents have traditional expectations for me. They're not trying to marry me off while I'm in high school or anything crazy, but they think there are certain things girls should do.

I don't have a lot of traditional interests. Like kids. In my culture there are a lot of kids. Everyone loves kids, except me. I don't hate kids. I even like babies because they'll sit on your lap and chew on a toy or something while you do something else. They're soft and warm. But once they start walking and getting into your stuff and whining and grabbing—ugh.

My mom takes care of my sisters' kids a lot. My mom and dad work. My sisters and their husbands work. Somehow everyone's schedules move around so someone's always taking care of the little kids. Of course, my brothers and me are supposed to help, too. But Bee and Toua get out of it way more than I do because they're boys. Even though they actually like playing with our nieces and nephew. Unlike me.

"I need to cook," my mom says, her knife flying across a pile of vegetables. She nods her head at the little kids peering over the edge of the table.

"Where's Bee?" I ask.

She shrugs.

I sigh and grab a couple of sticky little hands, pulling them into the other room.

"Play Hmong tag with us!" Lucky begs.

"Like Bee does!"

"I don't know how to say the whole thing," I mumble, even though that's not true.

"I know it!" Jalia says proudly. "My mom says it's an important part of our hair . . . hair . . ."

"Heritage," I say, rolling my eyes. Ever since my younger older sister, Song, started working at the Hmong arts organization, she's been all about Hmong culture. She's started calling me by my Hmong name even though she was the one who picked out Penny for my English name.

"Penny Lee—people will think you're white if they just see your name on paper," she said to me once.

In case you're wondering, "Hmong tag," as Lucky calls it, just uses a chant you say to decide who's it. Like eeny, meeny, miny, mo in English. You do this finger thing . . . with Bee and the kids, it always turns into a wrestling match.

My mom thinks Song's kids are kind of wild because Song listens to Hmong hip-hop and her husband takes the kids to b-boy battles. I think they're wild because they're little. And because Bee always gets them hyper when he's home. I'm not in the mood for hyper now. Or ever.

"I'm tired. How about you watch *Dora*," I say, grabbing the remote. There's some whining, but they settle down around me on the couch.

I tune out the annoying voices from the TV and pick up my flower cloth. I do like some traditional things, like sewing. It's not like I ever had a choice to learn—I was younger than Jalia when my mom and sisters taught me. But I'm good, really good. Song keeps saying Jalia wants me to teach her, but I don't have the patience. I can see Jalia now watching me out of the corner of her eye, and I feel kind of bad.

But this is not the time. Selling my flower and story cloths at my aunt's stand in the farmers' market is one of the ways I earn money for the Teg. The market will be opening again in a few weeks, and I want to have a lot of cloths ready. My cloths sell better than a lot of older women's because my designs are the best blend of old and new. Of course, no one says this, because they want me to be humble, but I know it.

See, it's not like I don't care about Hmong culture or history. I even cry sometimes at night thinking about what people in my family went through to get to the United States before I was born. One of the first story cloths I helped sew was my family's story of the refugee camp. But my parents don't get that Hmong kids are into other stuff now too. Like hip-hop and breaking. And cars.

I also make money doing homework for people other than Bee. Or more exactly, they pay to copy mine. In that case, it's not like I'm the smartest. Lots of my customers are plenty smart, like Johnny Xiong. They're just lazy, but they have money and they want to graduate, so they get enough from me to slide by in class. It's not very honest, and it's another thing my parents would kill me for, but they won't let me get a real job.

*We need you at home.*
*You focus on school.*
*Why do you need money anyway?*
They'd never understand.

# CHAPTER FIVE

The kids are glued to the TV, finally, so I sneak back out to the Teg to do Bee's math. It's the only place in the house (well, outside, I guess) that feels like it's private. Maybe Bee'll be home soon, and we can start installing the new valve guides.

I walk around the car, admiring how low we got it finally. I wanted the Teg totally slammed so the tires are tucking, no finger gap action here. If you're not careful, the car still scrapes sometimes.

I settle in the passenger's seat again,

flipping through Bee's notebook. A paper crane falls out. It's a note from a girl, of course. I won't read it. Bee knows I keep some private stuff in the glove compartment of the Teg, and he never messes with it. I'm tucking the crane back into his notebook when something written on the crane's wing catches my eye.

*X Rate, civic, $100, Mon 10—you in?*

*Dope.*

The second is Bee's handwriting. The first part—I'm not sure. It might be Yer Yang's writing. But I know right away what it means.

X Rate is what Johnny Xiong's older brother Chai calls himself. Too much being called Chai Tea in junior high, Toua said. Chai's been driving a Civic lately—he was working on it all winter, Johnny said.

Toua told me to stay away from Johnny because he's in a gang. But my brothers don't really like me talking to any guys. (I'm not sure how I'm supposed to get married and have lots more grandkids for my mom if I'm never allowed to date.) I'm not scared of Johnny—if he's in a gang, it's just because Chai is. I'm not friends with Johnny or anything, but we do have a business relationship. It's one way, though—I don't buy weed or anything else he's selling.

But Chai is something else. He graduated or left school last year, but I remember how people got out of his way in the halls. He got in trouble for bringing a box cutter to school. He got in a lot of fights. He's scary.

And my brother's going to race him for $100 on Monday.

# CHAPTER SIX

Bee's still not home by the time I finish our homework. I'm flipping through *Super Street* trying to decide about underglows when I hear the garage door open. It's just Toua. He knocks on the roof of the Teg and goes in the house.

He comes back out, backs out the minivan, and pulls his 300ZX in and opens the hood.

"I'm thinking about red," I say as I get out of the Teg.

He grunts, unhooking the work light to move it over. "Too many potholes in this city. You hit one the wrong way, bye-bye underglows. You got money to spend, let's talk about some JDM stuff. That's how you get respect."

I shrug. Some of the JDM stuff is cool looking, sure . . .

"How about JDM headlights? I know someone selling," Toua says, pointing at a torque wrench. I hand it to him.

"I thought those weren't safe in the U.S. because of driving on the other side of the road," I say.

Toua raises his eyebrows. "The Teg leaving the garage anytime soon? You sneaking out at night?"

I hit him automatically but feel my stomach clench.

"Do you know where Bee is?" I say casually.

Toua shakes his head. He's my brother, so I love him, but he's always bossed me and Bee around. No way I'm telling him about the note. Besides, I shouldn't have read it.

"Well, girls love underglows," Toua says, stretching and scratching his stomach. I hit him again. If underglows are girlie, I'm not getting them.

The door to the house opens, and this time it's my mom. I can tell from her look that I've been in the garage too long, never mind that I've mostly been doing homework. I hurry inside to be a good auntie until Song picks up the kids.

Bee and Toua walk in together right as I'm helping my mom put the food on the table. Everyone's basically quiet while we eat, just a few comments from my mom or dad about work or clan gossip.

After I help my mom clean up, I follow Bee out to the garage. I'm not going to say anything to him. I just want to see what I can figure out from talking to him. Maybe I'll bring up Johnny. Bee doesn't do the strict older brother thing as much as Toua.

Bee moves the work light back to the Teg and opens the garage door.

"Start her up," he says. "Need to tune some more."

He hooks up the laptop while I get in and

turn the key.

"Rev," he says from behind the hood. "Again."

We put the Teg through her paces. Bee looks dissatisfied as I get out.

"How much money do you have?" he asks.

"Nothing really. But the market opens soon, so I'll have more then. Plus—" I stop. I've never told anyone in my family that I let kids copy homework and sometimes tests for money. But either Bee has never looked at what flower cloths sell for and done the math or he doesn't care how I get money for the Teg parts.

"Plus what?"

"Nothing."

"You got another way of getting money?" Bee asks, looking at me hard. He looks angry. I feel scared. "I saw you talking to Johnny Xiong," he says before I can say anything. "You dealing for him?"

"What?!" I say. I feel like he's accused me of being a whore or something. I would never deal drugs. Would he?

He looks relieved. "Sorry," he says, putting

a hand on my shoulder. “I just worry that I got you into this,” he gestures at the Teg, “and it’s expensive. I don’t want you doing anything stupid for money. I’ve always got you covered, you know.” He bends back over the engine.

I’ve never asked him where he gets his money either. Everyone works for my aunt at the farmers’ market or picks vegetables sometime during the growing season, but nobody gets rich from what she pays. Toua and Bee are always buying or swapping cars and bikes and parts and reselling stuff, but I’m not sure how that works exactly.

“You’ve already gotten a lot of stuff for the Teg,” I say, and it’s true. If Bee thinks she needs something and I don’t have the money, he’s usually too impatient to wait until I do.

“Somebody was getting rid of it cheap,” he’ll say when he comes home with the part. Or “I traded some crap for it.”

“Anyway,” I say, “I don’t mind going slow with it. What’s the rush? I’ll have the money for it eventually, and someday Mom and Dad will have to let me get a job. Or I’ll marry someone rich," I joke.

I mean it about going slow with the Integra. That way Bee and I will have a long time to work on it together.

"So why were you talking to Johnny?" he says.

*Why are you and Toua always spying on me?* I complain in Hmong. Then I switch back to English. "I already come straight home from school every day, can't have a job, can't do extracurriculars without fighting with Mom. Can't you just let me have a life at school?" I surprise myself with how mad I sound.

Bee looks surprised too. *I'm just looking out for you. I'm your brother.*

I mutter something about Hmong guys. Bee snorts.

"You sound like Song's friends. I'm not marrying any fourteen-year-old girls, so don't get mad at me. It's not wrong to want your little sister to stay away from gang members. Go start the car again."

As I rev the engine, I wonder why he doesn't stay away from gang members.

# CHAPTER SEVEN

Bee is already working on the Teg when I get home from school on Friday. I look over his shoulder. He's got a turbo kit half installed. "Whoa! Where'd that come from?" I ask.

"Steve Thao—we're borrowing it for now. Just wanted to see how it works. I should have the money for it on Monday, though."

I feel the knot in my stomach again.

"Monday?" is all I can say.

Bee grunts. I wimp out. How can I ask about the race on Monday? Never mind what happened yesterday on Lexington Avenue.

Today in school rumors were flying about the kid who got hit, how bad he was hurt, if he was going to live. Cops were interviewing kids who saw it happen, everyone said. Pakou was super scared they'd want to talk to her. I knew I didn't have to tell her not to say anything about the Teg—she's had a crush on Bee forever. Besides, it wasn't our Teg anyway, right?

"I really will have more money once the market opens," I say, dumping my bag in the car. "You don't have to worry about it. I can pay Steve then. We're family, right? I'm sure he'd let us wait. Or we can give the turbo back until then—"

Bee interrupts. "Just because his cousin is married to our sister doesn't mean he's going to hold this for three weeks for us. He's already offering a good price. Don't worry about it. Like I said, I got you covered."

I watch him work for a minute, thinking about how long I heard him on the phone last night. Laughing softly and speaking more Hmong than he usually does in a week. I know it's that girl in California.

For a while now Toua's been teasing Bee about Fresno and "General VP's granddaughter." I really wasn't snooping—I just borrowed Bee's phone because my battery was dead, and he left the texts right there, like he wanted me to see them. I only glanced at them, but this girl wanted to know when Bee was moving to California.

Of course, I don't think she's really Vang Pao's granddaughter. General Vang Pao is, like, the most famous Hmong person ever. But there is some girl Bee's talking to and she isn't from around here or I would have heard about it. Somebody here probably introduced them, though—lots of Minnesota Hmong have family in California.

I wish Bee would like Pakou. Because she's my friend and because then he wouldn't be thinking about leaving after he graduates this year. Most people we know stay after high school. They go to college nearby or get a job. Another reason why I'm not in a rush to finish the Teg—anything I can do to keep him interested in stuff here. Maybe then he'll sign up for some community college classes

Bee breaks into my thoughts. "We should look at the list. See what you want to do next with all that money you're going to make soon." He's teasing, but it's a perfect chance.

I grab the notebook out of the glove compartment. There's a page for performance, one for sound, and one for looks. There are lots of drawings of cars and parts all over the covers. When Toua and Bee were younger, before they got cars, they loved drawing cars. Most of my friends were obsessed with learning how to draw girlie stuff and manga, but like my brothers, I spent most of my time trying to draw cars. We don't draw so much now, but sometimes it helps to picture a mod we're deciding about.

Bee's walking around the car, listing things on his fingers, just like our dad does.

"It's as low as it can go, the tires are tucking, the tires are pretty good—you might want to upgrade sometime, but—"

I interrupt. "I saw some Pirellis on another

Teg. They were sweet. I want to get some soon."

Bee looks surprised as I write it on the list. But he keeps going.

"We just upgraded to LED headlights last year—"

"Toua said I needed JDM stuff—he knows someone with headlights, but I don't think that's a good idea," I say.

Bee frowns, rubbing his face. "He's right," he says slowly. "The Teg won't be perfect without some JDM parts . . ." He stares at the car. "Put it on the list—I got to think about it."

"How about nitrous?" I say casually.

Now Bee looks really surprised. "You want to put in nitrous? Why?"

I shrug, doodling on the notebook. "It's cool." And it would take forever to install.

Bee stands in front of me. "Penny, I thought we were working hard to have you a sweet ride by the time you turn eighteen and get your license. But the Teg will be for getting you to school and stuff, letting you get out without having to rely on Mom and Dad. You're not going to be racing it . . . are you?"

He doesn't wait for me to answer. "No, you can't race. Who's going to teach you? And there aren't any tracks in town. And—no. Besides, you know what nitrous can do to an engine. Toua won't even put in nitrous and he—" Bee stopped.

"Toua races?" I ask, my voice getting squeaky.

Bee shrugs. "Just sometimes, with his friends. Not a big deal."

"Couldn't you guys teach me how to race?" I beg, even though I've never wanted to race. "After I get my license and I'm legal?"

Bee shook his head. "We're—" He stopped, his face still. "We're not those kind of brothers," he said, his voice sounding funny.

My heart was beating so hard, I could feel it in my hands. I just knew what he had been about to say: *we're leaving*.

# CHAPTER EIGHT

The more I thought about it over the weekend, the more it made sense that if Bee moved to California, Toua would go with him. When you come from a really close community where few people leave their families, it's scary to think about going someplace else alone. There's a Hmong saying that each person is a drop of water in a bucket—if the drop falls out of the bucket, it soon dries up.

Besides, Toua's just taking classes at Metro State, trying to get into the U, but he hasn't gotten in yet. There's nothing to hold him here either . . . except the rest of us.

I thought about screwing up Bee's homework so he wouldn't graduate, but that would be so low. It probably wouldn't work anyway since he usually doesn't have trouble passing tests. He's smart and knows enough of what's happening in class to get by. Besides, even if I did keep him from graduating, I can't see him repeating next year with me. He has his pride. He'd take the GED or just leave without a diploma and how would he ever get a good job? I could never do that to him.

My best hope is the Teg. Like I said, a car is never done. I could come up with projects for it and keep him busy over the summer. I could talk him into signing up for Metro State classes. Better still, the rest of the family could do that. My parents are big into education. And maybe the California girl would find someone else.

"You know," I say to Bee on Sunday. "I'm not going to get my license right on my birthday. I don't think the Teg will be close to done this summer, and there's no rush. Even if it's not done for school starting, that's OK. I like taking the bus with Pakou. You know Pakou, the cute one?"

Bee stares at me, wiping his hands on a rag and then automatically wiping the engine. "Of course I know Pakou, *the skinny one*—she's been your best friend since Jackson. She's annoying. Talks too much."

I think sourly about all the time he spent talking to California girl. She's the one who talks too much.

"And it will be done for your birthday in June," Bee continues grimly. "And you're taking your test then too. Don't worry, I'll take you out to practice before that."

"Well, it's not a big deal to me," I say carefully. "And I've been adding onto the list. We haven't really done much with the stereo. Oh, and I got a great idea—I want a five-point belt and I'm going to embroider it."

Bee looks confused by all these new ideas. I've been going through the magazines in the garage all weekend making my list. Except for the embroidery one. That's all mine, and I'm actually kind of excited about it.

"Embroider—what?" Bee asks.

"Well, I could just do a pattern with something traditional like elephant's foot, or I could do like a story cloth."

"You mean, like the story of the Hmong leaving Laos and the war and refugee camps and stuff?" Bee frowns.

I pick at a hangnail. "Umm, actually I was thinking the story of this car, the story of how we've worked on it."

This was what I really want to do, but I don't want Bee to think it was stupid. The Hmong have always saved our stories in the pictures in our sewing. I'm going to do everything I could to keep Bee here, but even if he doesn't move, I know that things wouldn't be the same as we get older. I want to remember the time we'd had together and put it down in thread.

But Bee doesn't laugh. He clears his throat. "That would make the Teg more awesome and unique than anything we can buy." Then he does laugh. "Plus, I really want to see you do car parts in reverse appliqué or whatever that stuff is you do."

"If I can draw it, I can sew it," I say.

"Hey, are you sure you haven't been listening to Mom? This kind of sewing might have Hmong guys lining up around the house to marry you."

I smack him on the arm.

# CHAPTER NINE

I'm tense all day Monday, waiting for night. I don't run into Bee at school, not even lunch, which is weird. But he's home after school. I show him some sketches I did during class of my ideas for the harness, and he says they're cool.

"The harness with parts will be about a hundred bucks," says Bee. "I've got that hundred bucks now I said I'd have today—do you want to go get one?"

"You've got it now?" I say, taken aback. I thought the hundred bucks was coming from the race tonight. *Mon 10* the note had said.

"Yeah," says Bee looking at me funny and looking a little nervous too. "I don't think this turbo of Steve's is going to work anyway. If we get the harness now, you can be working on it while I'm working on other stuff for the Teg to have it ready in time."

My mind's spinning with other thoughts, but it snags on the last part he said.

"In time?" I say, raising my voice. "In time for *what*?! I keep telling you I don't care about my birthday and I don't want to rush it. I just want things to be perfect. Whose car is it, anyway? Mine or yours?"

Bee's mouth hangs open. I've probably only yelled at him a few times ever and not since we were a lot younger. Then his face gets tight.

"I'm just trying to do something nice for your *birthday*," he says stiffly. "Forget it." He walks toward the house door. I grab his arm.

"OK, I'm sorry, I'm sorry," I babble. I can't stand to fight with him. It's not like I can tell him what I'm really mad about: that he's thinking about leaving. That he's racing. That he might have killed someone. Me being a witch isn't going to fix any of that.

"Let's go look at harnesses now," I say. "I'll pay you back."

He flips his hand like *don't worry about it* and pulls out his keys.

Bee wants to check out a new shop he heard about in Hopkins. It's only a few blocks from our house to 94, but before we even get there he's pushing fifty on the city streets.

"God, slow down!" I yell, grabbing my door. Bee just laughs.

As soon as we're on the highway, the Teg is flying. As Bee swerves around another sad commuter like he's standing still, I hear an exhaust as loud as ours coming up from behind.

A Civic pulls up on our left. Some Asian guys inside are gesturing at us. Bee throws them the finger and slams down on the gas.

"Who was that?" I ask, my hands clenched.

"Losers," he answers as we get off at our exit.

On the way home, fingering the cherry-red harness in my lap, I get suspicious.

"You didn't get this to make sure I was busy with *women's work* so you could do all the fun stuff on the car, did you?" I ask.

Bee laughs. "I know you can swing a wrench better than a lot of guys. Didn't Toua and I teach you? You can work on whatever you want. It's your car, after all."

That night I keep track of where Bee is in the house so he can't sneak out without me knowing. At nine thirty he's in the garage on the phone. I'm sitting in the kitchen, looking out the window at his car on the street. Everyone will hear if he opens the garage door to take the Teg or Honda. The minivan's parked on the street too, right now, but he's hardly taking that.

Ten o'clock and I can still hear him in the garage.

"School night," my mom says.

"I still have homework," I mumble, picking up a book.

At ten thirty my parents go to bed, telling

me I need to sleep soon.

"And tell Bee to go to bed too," Dad says.

I can hear Bee laughing. Then he comes in the house. He's surprised to see me.

"If it's my homework, forget it," he says. "Go to bed."

"Soon," I say.

Bee goes to his and Toua's room. I turn off the light and stay in the kitchen. No one can leave the house without me seeing. I stare out the window at Bee's car. Eleven, twelve. I put my head down on my notebook. The race, it must have been today during school. Monday 10 A.M.

# CHAPTER TEN

For the next week I watch Bee and work on my harness embroidery. Bee's acting mostly normal, and my harness is starting to look really awesome. Bee laughs when he sees how I put him in with the hat he likes to wear and his orange shoes.

I'm feeling better too, because the kid who got hit is getting better, people say. Might be going home soon.

But Bee hasn't been at school every day. Or not all of every day. By Sunday I've decided I need to know where he's going and what's going on. Is he racing more? Why? To get money to go to California?

If he's racing, sooner or later he'll get in trouble. If he's doing something stupid like racing because of that girl, it makes me even madder. I want Bee to stay in Minnesota, but staying here because he's in jail isn't the way I planned it. I need to see for myself if he's racing.

On Monday, I ask Bee to give me a ride to school. After I say good-bye to him and act like I'm going to my locker, I walk right out the back door of the school. I'm hoping Bee will stay at school for at least first period so he won't get marked absent right away. I walk to a bus stop away from school and go home.

I hold my breath as I open the garage door. No one's cars are there, but I'm still scared that my mom or dad will pop out of the house door. It's quiet.

I close the hood of the Integra. Last night I made sure we took the Integra for a test drive so she would be drivable today. I'm pretty sure I could fix anything Bee might have taken apart, but I don't have the time today.

There's no way to drive the Teg quietly. I find the *grum, grum* exhaust noise soothing. It's a good thing that lots of people around here want their cars to sound loud. No one notices me.

I can see Bee's car in the lot still so I park on the street by the school. I shove all my hair up into a plain black winter hat. I settle in.

I wait a long, long time. I wish I had brought something to read. I can hear any cars leaving the lot, and I know I'll hear Bee's car—it's loud too.

I've closed my eyes and am dozing when I hear it. My eyes flip open, and I slouch down in the seat. Bee turns the other direction so I start the Teg. I'm panicking about how to follow him. I don't want to lose him, but I don't want to be stopped too close to him at a light, either. I hear him turn onto Lexington, so I gun it and just make the light.

There are a bunch of cars between us, so I feel safe. Bee gets on the highway, and I wonder where he's going. All the racing I've heard about is in the city. He drives a long way out.

When he exits the highway, I hang way back. I start to get nervous that the Teg will be noticeable. I let him get far ahead of me . . . and I lose him. He turned somewhere into one of the suburban subdivisions and I missed it.

I drive around a little bit, looking. There's hardly anyone on the streets around here. I get to a section of county highway that's going through empty land with some farmland. I realize that this is the first time I've been out in the Teg by myself. Seeing the open and empty road in front of me, I have a sudden desire to floor it.

The speed wipes my mind clean of all my worries. I even forget why I'm out in the Teg. All that time spent working on the Teg and tinkering with the engine, I never thought a lot about speed in a real way. Bee and Toua must have. They take the Teg out without me sometimes, maybe they've even raced it, though until recently I didn't think they did that. Now I'm racing all alone and it's awesome. Racing doesn't seem so stupid anymore.

I look at the clock. It's almost lunch at school. I'm not finding Bee today, so I should get back to school with the late excuse I wrote and signed my mom's name to.

I make it back home in almost half the time it took to get out to wherever Bee's going. The highway traffic is light in the middle of the day, and every chance I get, I let the Teg rip. It's like the good girl part of me is back at school. The Teg has a fuzz buster, but that only tells you if a cop is using a radar gun to check your speed. If a cop is on the highway, I'm done since I don't have a license. That does scare me a little but not enough to stop me.

# CHAPTER ELEVEN

I put the Teg in the garage, pop the hood, run to catch the bus, and make it back to school after lunch. The secretary takes my note, and I slide into math class.

The next day I persuade Bee to let me drive his car to school.

"You said you'd help me practice for my test," I say sweetly.

I park his Nissan where I'll be able to see it throughout the day. When I look out the door before lunch, it's gone. I curse. I don't know when he left so I don't know what to do.

It's like a cat-and-mouse game the rest of the week. I try to get the rhythm of when Bee's leaving, but it's not predictable. I keep telling myself he could be skipping to do lots of things besides racing. Most racing happens on weekend nights, right? But I can't think of anything good he can be doing.

I'm obsessed. And I'm itching to drive the Teg again alone. I could skip out of school any day and go do it, but I won't let myself without a good reason. Keeping Bee here and out of trouble is a good reason, I tell myself.

It's time to try some other things, things I thought I'd never do. Snooping and Johnny Xiong. Snooping's easy since Bee trusts me with his school stuff and thinks I leave his private things alone. I shake out every notebook and textbook and go through his bag. I find a few notes from girls and I read them, looking for any clues. Nothing, except this in a note from Lucy Lor: *I heard you've got a hunny in Cali—true?? Too bad 4 all the MN girls . . .*

Bee hadn't written anything back on her note.

I think about getting his phone to go through his texts, but that would be harder. So I talk to Johnny.

My brothers are overprotective, but I do think they're right about Johnny. Pakou says he stares at me all the time in class, so maybe he does like me. He sure spends a lot of money to copy my answers. And he is in a gang.

On Monday Johnny comes to my locker before school to borrow my math notebook.

"Is there going to be a rematch?" I ask casually, taking his smoky, cologne-y smelling money.

Johnny looks confused. "What?"

"You know, between Bee and Chai," I say, my heart thudding.

Johnny rolls his eyes. "Chai's gotten beat three times, so you'd think that would be enough, but it's turning into a grudge match. That's a sweet car your brother's got. I hear you've got an even sweeter one, though." He grins, leaning closer.

I blush. Most people don't know the Teg is mine. Bee must be talking.

"So, I've been there," I say, looking in my locker. "But I don't remember where you go after you get off the highway."

"It's easy," Johnny says, turning my math notebook over and sketching a map on the back. "Why? You going to the one today? I could give you a ride."

I shrug as the bell rings. I hurry off to homeroom to get marked present for the day. During passing time, I walk out the door and catch the bus home.

As I drive out to the race site, I keep glancing at the map on my phone, studying the area around it. I need a place I can watch from. After I exit the highway, I circle around, getting to know the area, avoiding the street Johnny put on the map. There is a little subdivision of identical houses but, after that, just county roads surrounded by fields.

It's deserted, no other cars once I'm past the houses. I circle closer and turn off onto a road parallel to the one used for racing. The road I'm on is on the top of a hill. The racing road is down below. I pull the Teg off onto the shoulder and get out. I walk into a field until I can see the racing road below.

There's nobody here. I sit down in the dirt, wondering what I'll say if a farmer comes along in a tractor. Just run for it, I guess.

It's breezy and still cold. Spring in Minnesota. But the sun feels warm on my shoulders as I rest my chin on my knees, hugging them to me. Maybe the race happened already. Maybe Johnny was wrong about it being today.

I check my phone. Only 9:40. School starts so stupid early it's easy to forget that most people are just starting their day now. I bet Chai Xiong doesn't get up at 5:30.

Then I hear them, the farting grumming noise of the exhaust and engines. I almost jump up, but then I realize I need to stay out of view. If I don't do anything stupid, they shouldn't see me.

I pick out Bee's Nissan right away. There are six other cars I don't recognize. One of them's a Teg, different color than mine though. They stop below me, and some people get out. I can't hear them, but I can see Bee leaning out of his window, the hat he always wears. One of the cars takes off again down the road. To block the other end? It sinks in as I look at the road. One of the cars will be driving in the oncoming traffic lane. I suck in my breath.

After a few minutes of people milling around, Bee's car and a sweet Toyota Supra move up. Bee's on the wrong side of the road. A girl stands between the cars, her hand up. Her long hair blows in the wind, and she drops her hand.

The Nissan and the Supra shoot past her, the Supra a little ahead. I jump up to see better without realizing what I'm doing. Trees and a curve block my view. The other cars are pulling out now too, following the racers.

I hold my breath long after all the cars are gone. I can barely hear them. I don't hear any crash sounds. Would I? I wait a long time. They must have just left by the other end of the road. I slowly walk back to the Teg.

Now I've seen it for myself. Bee's racing.

Bee's racing during the day. Bee's racing during the day on regular roads in ways that he or other people could get hurt.

Now I know. He could have been one of the racers the day the kid got hit on Lexington.

# CHAPTER TWELVE

Someone has to know who was racing that day, I'm sure. I could ask Johnny, but that doesn't feel right. Those other people who came to watch the race, they might know. Like I said, most races are at night and lots of people come just because it's the fun thing to do. But these races in the middle of the schoolday and workday, way out of the city—they seem like something different. And the people there must be the hard-core street racers. I guess that includes my brother now.

I push the thought away. I need to find

those people. I'm not too worried about talking to them. It's not my style usually, but I can BS. Especially if I can see these people without Bee around. But in case he is, I'm going to need a disguise.

It takes the rest of the week to get everything together.

"You have any lipstick and stuff I can have?" I ask my oldest sister when I'm at her house on Sunday. If I can avoid spending any of my money on this stuff, I want to. It's not like I'll need any of it later.

Sherry (as she calls herself these days) acts like she's going to fall over.

"Are you really going to start acting more like a girl than a boy now? No more hiding in the garage?" she screeches. "Who's the lucky guy? Wait, it isn't Johnny Xiong, is it? You know he's in a gang, right?"

I roll my eyes. She's been bugging me to let her do a makeover since I started high school.

"I can make you look so different," she says, pushing me into a chair. Her kids crowd around, giggling. Normally I would be insulted but that's exactly what I want.

Before I leave, I rummage in Sherry's closet for some clothes. She's got so many, she won't notice.

"What are you doing?"

I jump, my face is totally guilty. I drop the skirt I'm holding.

Sherry picks it up. "You want this? Who are you, and what did you do with my sister?"

"Uhhh, uhh, it's for . . ." Why can't I think of a lie??

She outs her hand on my arm. "You could just ask. It's totally time you start thinking about these things even if Mom and Dad still think of you as a little kid."

I mumble something and get away as fast as I can, clutching the clothes.

I wash my face as soon as I get home and hide all the stuff in my underwear drawer.

Pakou, wide-eyed, hands over some boots on the bus.

"Are you really going to wear them?" she asks. "You just always wear sneakers. Is this because of Johnny? I heard he might ask you to prom."

I stuff the boots in my backpack. Johnny and prom is bad news, but I don't have time to think about that either.

Now that I have everything, it's time to get sick.

# CHAPTER THIRTEEN

On Monday morning I don't get up. I have my eyes closed when I feel my mom touching me. I moan.

*What's wrong?!* she asks.

*I don't feel good*, I say, sighing. She calls my dad in. *Wait!* I say, sitting up a little. *I don't need the shaman or anything.*

*She's never sick!* Mom says to Dad. *Do a soul calling.*

My dad finishes buttoning his shirt and nods. It takes some fast-talking to convince them I'm not that sick, but I can't go to school either. Finally, they decide to leave me home, but my mom's getting herbal medicine for me on the way home. Whatever.

As soon as the door closes after my parents, I throw off my pajamas. I yank on the short skirt and T-shirt I got from Sherry and top it with one of her sexy little jackets. I stick my feet into Pakou's boots and zip them up. So far, so good. I already look like a stranger.

I heat up my mom's curling iron as I put on makeup in the bathroom. Good thing Sherry doesn't go for a natural look. I paint my eyelids green with a little streak of pink thrown in. Eyeliner changes me even more. Blush and then some plum-purple lipstick. I draw a mole on my cheek with the eyeliner. I'm getting carried away.

I brush out my hair and start curling pieces for that loose, long curl look. (I usually wear my hair in a ponytail.) I wish I could have orange streaks—it seems like the kind of thing this girl I'm dressing up as would have. *I'll just say I'm too traditional*, I think, giggling. It's weird to admit, but I'm having fun.

I close my eyes as I walk into my room. I open them when I think I've shuffled in front of the mirror. Wow. WOW! I look pretty. Well, not exactly pretty because the makeup is freaky and the skirt is a little skanky for me but . . . I've never looked so girlie or at least not since I was a kid.

I'm satisfied Bee will never recognize me, maybe not even if he looks right at my face (which I'll make sure he doesn't do). First, he'll never expect to see me there. Second, I know it's a racist thing that people say all Asians look alike. That's stupid, but there ARE a lot of short Hmong girls with long black hair. In different clothes with a different hairstyle, I'll blend right in.

I'm giddy as I run out the door. I'm saving so much time by not going to school. Plus my mom called in a real excuse for me, so I don't even have to worry. As the Teg roars to life, I think I can feel her excitement about what we're going to do today too. Maybe the Teg's wanted a bad girl all along.

We fly down the highway, changing lanes

just for the fun of flashing around other cars just like Bee does, even though it's rush hour. Things slow down around downtown. I drum my fingers on the steering wheel as I think about my strategy. I look at the map again on my phone, looking for good stakeout positions.

I end up on my high road again, farther along. I sit in the car for a while, listening to the engine tick. Was it stupid to rush out here? I didn't want to miss my chance. I listen to music for a while, keeping it down. I'm straining to hear their engines.

I get out a couple of times to stretch my legs and because it's sunny, but the cold air creeping around my shivering knees and thighs drives me back in the car. How do girls wear these kinds of skirts all the time?

Finally I hear it, the grumble, the fart, the gearshifts. I start the Teg, foot ready as I watch. As soon as they go by, I shoot out, skidding onto the county road. I catch them before they turn onto the racing road. I don't see Bee's car in the five ahead of me. My hands are sweating as I pull in right on a Civic's tail.

Doors open immediately and people spill out. More than last time maybe. I take a deep breath. Someone here knows about that day. I get out.

I walk up to one of the groups of people. There's a girl—good.

"Hi!" I say, trying to channel Pakou through her boots. Bee's right—she talks a lot. She's very bubbly, and that's what I need now. "I thought Mai was going to be here," I chatter to the girl. Mai's a super-common Hmong girl name, so it seems safe. "I thought she said Pao might race today." I'm getting into it—I can already picture Mai and Pao, my imaginary cousins.

The girl looks me over. "You know Mai?" she asks.

"I'm her cousin from Wisconsin," I say, giggling.

"Where in Wisconsin?" she asks. I can tell we're about to play "do you know . . . ?" so I'm relieved when I hear another car coming. I hope it isn't Bee.

"There's Mai," the girl says as a Teg pulls up. It's the one from last time.

"Oh, that's the wrong—" I start to say, but the girl doesn't hear me.

She asks, "Is it because she's your cousin that your car looks exactly like Mai's?"

# CHAPTER FOURTEEN

"But it doesn't," I say stupidly. "Mine's red and hers is black."

The girl raises her eyebrows. "She just got hers repainted a few weeks ago—didn't you know?"

I shake my head trying to clear it. I have to keep a handle on this. "Oh, and, I mean, that's not my cousin. Wrong Mai!" I giggle nervously.

The girl's still looking at my Teg. She starts to walk toward it.

"Can I see?" she says over her shoulder.

"What's on the harness? Oh my god, is that embroidery?" She pulls the door open. "Wow, you are so good. My mom tried to teach me, but I suck. Who's that guy in the pictures?"

My mouth is hanging open, and my brain is filled with every swear word I know in Hmong or English.

"My, my boyfriend. I mean, it's not finished," I say. Now others are coming over, including Mai.

"Pop the hood," a guy says.

I never thought about the show-off-your-car part. My hands are shaking. I've got nothing to be ashamed of. I know this car. I'm just having a hard time being the me who worked on the Teg and the girl in the tight skirt and Pakou's boots. I glance at Mai—she seems to be both kinds of girls unless her Teg is her boyfriend's project.

I try not to stand like I'm giving a school report as I answer people's questions. The girl I was talking to is showing Mai the harness. Mai is frowning.

The guys agree I should get nitrous, and

then they pull away to talk macho smack before racing. Some of them get into a car and take off down the road, just like last time.

I drift over to the girls again uncertainly.

"What are they racing for?" I ask, trying to think of a way to bring up the hit-and-run race on Lexington.

"Slips," the not-Mai girl says as two cars pull up into the starting spots.

"Angie!" one of the guys yells, waving her over. The not-Mai girl (Angie) saunters over to stand between the cars as the guys gun their engines. She knows how to wear a short skirt and not feel stupid, you can tell. I tell myself to stop pulling on mine.

"So, do you race?" Mai says, all snotty.

"Uhhh—" I don't have to answer because Angie drops her hand and the roar from the cars is deafening. The guys start piling into cars. "Don't we go to see the finish?" I ask.

Mai flips her hair dismissively. "They'll be back."

We're quiet a minute. I'm scared of her, but I came here to find out what happened that day. And a Teg that used to be my Teg's twin . . .

It's like she can read my mind. "You've got Pirellis too," she says, still sounding aggressive. "How'd you get the idea to do that needlework on your harness?" She takes a step toward me, getting in my space.

"Uh, I just, just thought of it," I stammer. "Why—" But then over her shoulder through her driver's side window I see something on her harness. What the—?

Angie's sauntering back toward us, laughing over her shoulder at one of the guys who's still here. I wish she'd hurry up. I feel like Mai's about to hit me. I've never been in a fight before and while wearing these clothes doesn't feel like a good time to start.

"And that's Bee Lee in those pictures, isn't it?!" Mai hisses in my face. I take two steps back until I stumble into my Teg.

Angie glances in the window of Mai's car as she comes toward us.

"Oh my god!" she screeches again. "Why didn't you say that you're embroidering your harness too, Mai? Is this like the new Hmong girl thing? How come nobody told me? Just because I suck at sewing doesn't mean I couldn't get a homie to help me out, make me cool . . ."

"You know Bee?" I ask Mai quietly, my heart pounding.

Mai shrugs, smirking at me. "Maybe." She raises a penciled eyebrow.

But I already know the answer—the similarities between our cars can't just be coincidence. Bee must be the connection. I have to know what she knows.

# CHAPTER FIFTEEN

"I'll race you," I say, hardly believing the words as they come out of my mouth. "For information."

"Done," Mai says, tossing her keys at me and catching them on one long fingernail just as I flinch. "Whoever wins asks the questions and gets the answers. No lying."

"No lying," I agree, my entire body buzzing.

"What are you—" Angie's words as she walks toward us are drowned out by the returning cars.

I get in my Teg, trying to take deep breaths as Mai explains to the others what's going on. I don't know what reason she gives—she laughs as she talks, but the look she gives me as she gets in her Teg is pure and serious hate.

The other cars move out of the way as we pull up. I'm already on the right side so I stay there. If we meet an oncoming car, it won't really matter where I am, but it still feels safer.

One of the guys knocks on my window. I lower it.

"T's down at the end making sure it's clear, and you gotta hope no one comes out of a driveway. You know the road?"

I shake my head.

He lets out a whistle, and his eyes widen behind his funky glasses. "OK, you should just know it curves twice. The finish is the red mailbox on the right side, about half a mile away. Mai said it's a grudge match between Tegs. You know the terms you're racing on?"

I nod.

"OK, may the best girl win." He knocks on

my roof, and I raise the window.

Mai revs her engine, not like a macho guy but like a pilot getting ready for takeoff. But the whole time she's staring at me coolly. I rev my engine too. The Teg sounds sweet. She's been waiting for this day. We won't let each other down. I give Mai and the guy in the glasses a nod. He raises his hand.

When his hand falls, time lengthens. I suddenly feel cool and sure. My hands and feet know where to go, what to do. For the first few seconds, my body feels liquid as the Teg flies down the road and I shift in perfect rhythm. I feel like I *am* the Teg, and it's the best feeling ever. My eyes are on the first curve—it's far ahead but getting closer fast.

It's not until I finally take a breath again that I glance over at Mai. She's right there, like our cars are tied together by an invisible thread. She looks grim. I laugh out loud. Right now I feel so good doing this, I don't even care what happens.

Then we're on the curve, and the laugh dies in my mouth. It's a curve to the left, and it's steeper than I thought. I'm fighting to hold the Teg to the road. I'm still filled with the thrill of the speed, but whatever that part of your brain is that doesn't want you to get hurt or die is back, and I'm scared now too. And now Mai pulls ahead with the advantage the curve gave her.

The gear feels wrong. I downshift, trying to catch up. Curve again, now to the right. I wish I could close my eyes to think for a moment how to make it work for me. But I can't close my eyes—I'm driving. Oh god.

*Don't overthink it*, I hear Bee's voice say. Is he here? In my mind? This is starting to feel like such a dream, I'm not sure, and I can't look at anything but the road.

I let my hands and feet do as they want. It's all I can do.

Coming out of the second curve, I've caught up. I see cars ahead. Now—I have to do it now!

With my pedal to the floor and a death grip on the wheel, we flash past the cars and guys waving. It takes a moment to realize that Mai has stopped. I can only pull my foot slowly off the pedal, my legs shaking. No way could I slam on the brakes now.

When I'm going a normal speed, I turn around and drive slowly back to Mai and the guys. I have no idea what happened, who won. I feel like I'm going to throw up, there's so much adrenaline in my body.

I pull up next to Mai. Before I can get out, she's pulling open my door and yanking me out by my arm. She's cussing me out, and I keep saying "Who won?" Is she mad because I did?

"You're going to answer my questions!" she yells, not letting go of my arm.

"But—" I say.

"Ooooh, catfight, catfight!" the guys chant. I look for the glasses guy. I don't see him. The guys are just a blur anyway. "Settle it with a fight!" One of them whoops.

"Wait, did we tie?" I ask Mai, pulling away from her. She cusses at me some more. "I'll answer your questions," I say. "As long as you answer mine."

"Aren't you a skanky man-stealer?!" she yells at me.

"Nooo," I say, completely taken aback. What is she talking about? "Weren't you racing when that kid got hit on Lexington?" I shoot back.

"No!" she yells. "I don't even know what you're talking about!" But I see fear in her eyes. "And that's bullcrap what you said. That's Bee Lee in your embroidery, and he's my sister's boyfriend!"

"Wait, what?!" I say. "But what about the California gir—"

"So you knew! *My* sister is in California, but she's coming next week. You knew he had a girlfriend, and you went for him anyway, you—"

The guys are around us, clapping and laughing. But then one of them is pushing between us.

"OK, ladies, break it up, break it up. The dude's not worth it, I'm sure. Settle it another day with another race."

Oh, no. It's Bee.

# CHAPTER SIXTEEN

I turn my head, swinging my hair to hide my face. I start to walk away, but Mai grabs my arm again.

"Bee! Who is this b—"

Bee's looking past me to my Teg. He looks back at me, my head hanging down.

"Penny?!" His mouth stays open.

"And who's Penny?" Mai hisses, looking back and forth between us.

"Sister," Bee and I say at the same time. Now Mai's mouth falls open. I can't help it, I just start laughing.

# CHAPTER SEVENTEEN

After everyone's calmed down (now I'm just hiccuping. I feel like a five-year-old), I hold my breath and ask Mai the big question. I have to ask her. I still can't ask Bee.

"Was that your car that day even if you weren't driving?"

"What day?" Bee asks, confused.

She hesitates, exhales, and nods. "*My* brother was driving."

A huge weight lifts off my heart. At the same time, I'm sad for her. I know what that weight is like.

"Don't tell anyone," she begs me. I nod. I was never trying to get anyone in trouble, just trying to keep my brother. Mai doesn't want to lose her brother either. "That's why I painted it, got new plates, and he went to California," she continues in a low voice to me. "And that's why my sister's coming here. My brother will take her job with our uncle, and she'll help me take care of our grandparents."

"Kao Li's really coming here?" Bee says. I think it's the only part of the conversation he's understood. A grin is spreading across his face. Maybe it's just the only part he really cared about.

Mai nods, giving him a hard look. "And you'd better treat her right. Now you know how tough I am."

Bee laughs and tries to hide it.

"But if they get married, her name will be Kao Li Lee," I say behind my hand to Mai. "Are you sure you want that for your sister?"

She giggles. "Sounds like a good match for Bee Lee? They'll be perfect together."

Bee and I reach home at the same time.

I pull the Teg into the garage. Bee pulls his 300ZX in next to it. When I get out, he's standing there with folded arms.

"We need to talk," he says, sounding just like our dad. I don't know whether to laugh or cry. I'm so relieved he won't be leaving and he wasn't part of the race on Lexington. But I wish he wouldn't race like that at all. And I don't want to explain what I've been up to.

"First, what is up with all . . . that?" He points at me.

I shrug. "Sherry wanted to do a makeover. And . . . I didn't want you to recognize me. I'm going back to my old clothes—they're more comfortable. I kind of like the hair though."

Bee shakes his head like he's trying to clear it.

"OK, second, what the heck were you doing there? Why aren't you in school? Or in bed? Didn't you tell Mom you were sick?" He's being such a bossy older brother I get mad.

"Well, what were YOU doing there today? And all the other days you've skipped school to go do something stupid like race on a road where you or someone innocent could get hurt or killed? Huh?"

Bee shakes his head again. "You look so crazy, I can't even look at you. You don't even look like Penny."

"That's right, change the subject," I mutter, wiping my lipstick off with the back of my hand.

"But you're right," Bee says, looking at the Teg. "I don't know how you found out—was it Johnny? I didn't want you to know because I knew you wouldn't like it. And it was for you."

"For me?" I'm dumbfounded.

"Well, mostly. To win money to help you finish the Teg for your birthday."

"I TOLD you I don't care about finishing for my birthday!" I yell. "I never asked you for money! I can get my own money in perfectly safe and legal ways. Well, mostly legal," I finish, thinking about my homework business.

"I know, I know, and that why I didn't want you to know," Bee says, looking at me finally. "But it's important to me that you have the Teg for your birthday, Penny."

"Because you're leaving after all," I say, my eyes filling with tears. "With that skank Kao Li—"

"Whoa, whoa," Bee says, holding up a hand. "Kao Li is way more like you than she is like Mai. Even Mai's just playing dress up—she's a good kid too. And who said I'm leaving? It's just—I'm graduating—"

"Unless you flunk for skipping all the time," I put in.

Bee waves his hand. "I've already got enough credits. Plus, my homework always gets good grades." He smiles. "Listen, I'm graduating. I'll have to take some kind of community college classes because Mom and Dad will make me. But mostly I'm going to be really busy with my new job." He grins again.

"What new job?" I ask.

"Working on Formula Drift cars. That Hopkins guy with the new shop is working for the circuit and said he'd give me a try."

"Wow." I'm impressed. All those races we've watched together on YouTube and now Bee will be working on those cars.

"So I won't be around as much. And next year you'll graduate and go away to a fancy school," he continues.

"No, I won't," I counter.

"Well, you should if you can," Bee retorts. "Family should support you, not hold you back. You can always come home, but you need to make your own future."

I look down, trying not to cry again.

"And I promise I won't street race again. You're right, it's stupid. I just got sucked in because I usually win and it's an easy way to make money. But from now on I'll keep my racing to the track. I can kick Chai Xiong's butt just as easily there, take his money, and make him drive two hours for the privilege. Anyway, there's a rumor a track might be built in the metro."

"That would be sweet," I say, rubbing my hand on the hood of the Teg.

Bee raises his eyebrows.

"I mean," I say quickly, "it *is* stupid, but it was really . . . awesome. Really, really awesome."

"Now you know why me and Toua never taught you how to race. We didn't want you to catch the bug. But from what I saw today, you're a natural. Must be in the blood. Lees for speed."

As Bee puts his hand out for a high five, I know I'll never lose him, no matter where life takes us.

# THE ACURA INTEGRA

## MODEL HISTORY

Also known in markets outside the United States as the Honda Integra, this model has a lot in common with the Honda Civic. The Integra was a luxury sports car that was in production from 1985 to 2006. It was only available in front wheel drive, either in a two-door coupe or a four-door sedan style.

There have been four generations of Integras to enter the market. Many owners "soup up" their vehicles (add parts to make them more visually appealing or sporty). One of the most common "mods" (modifications) made is the installation of a cold air intake system. Since engines thrive off colder air, these systems help ramp up the horsepower of a vehicle.

Some Integra owners also supercharge, or turbocharge, their engines. The job of a turbocharger is to force more air through the engine at a faster rate. The more air that moves through the engine and the faster it moves, the more power can be exerted from the automobile.

Honda Formula 1 cars were the predecessors of the Integra. The Integra has been active in racing circles ever since its introduction in the 80s.

## THE INTEGRA TYPE R

First released in 1995, this car was named "the greatest front-wheel-drive performance car ever" by *Evo* magazine. This car was considered to have superior handling, acceleration, and performance as compared to other Honda models.

The Type R vehicle was produced mainly for publicity purposes. Honda hoped that the car's performance in international racing circles would win it support on the commercial market. Their upgrades paid off, and Type R was very competitive on the racetrack.

The Type R had a five-speed manual transmission and better intake and exhaust systems than the original Acura Integra. With increased power and a lighter overall weight, the Integra Type R was built to move fast.

## THE INTEGRA AND THEFT

While the Integra was often ranked among lists of the most stolen vehicles in the United States, it wasn't stolen as much as its cousin, the Honda

Civic. The Integra, like the Civic, was a popular target for thieves because it was relatively easy to break into and because its parts were in high demand and could be used on many different makes and models of vehicles.

## THE INTEGRA TODAY

The Integra today is a scooter. I'm not kidding! Honda has done this before—converted a car model into a motorcycle model. In fact, according to jalopnik.com, the Integra was actually a motorcycle model before it became a car model in 1985. Regardless, Honda claims that the new 2013 Honda Integra has great handling and comfort, combining the power and performance of a motorbike with the ease of a scooter.

# PENNY'S ACURA INTEGRA

***ENGINE:*** 140 horsepower, 1.8-liter transverse front-wheel-drive engine, valve train—four valves per cylinder (sixteen in total); a turbo kit to ramp up the horsepower and max RPM; replaced valve guides (the Teg needed new ones because the engine was starting to burn oil—not good); installed a cold air intake system (engines like cold air, which increases the vehicle's horsepower); installed a new five-point belt (with my one-of-a-kind embroidery to boot); replaced fuel injectors

***DRIVETRAIN:*** replaced ball joints; cut down the manual shifter to a short shifter (makes it quicker to transition from one gear to another and helps the Teg accelerate faster)

***SUSPENSION:*** replaced the front sway bar and rear sway bar; installed Integra coilovers (drops the Teg low to the ground—with a lower center of gravity, the car will handle and perform better on the road); camber kit (shock absorber that helps straighten out the wheels and makes for a smoother ride)

***BRAKES:*** new front and rear brake pads; installed rotors (these keep the brakes cool, letting out the heat produced by braking—cooler brakes last longer and stop more efficiently)

***WHEELS/TIRES:*** Pirelli tires (like the ones Mai had—they looked so sleek I just had to get them!); tucked tires; trimmed bumper and quarter panels to prevent rubbing or friction

***EXTERIOR:*** replaced LED headlights with JDM (Japanese Domestic Market) headlights; painted the body with a fresh red coat; installed underglows; tinted the windows; installed an ITR back spoiler (increased downforce, which enhances tire traction—important for a fast-moving front-wheel-drive car)

***INTERIOR:*** added a superior-handling steering wheel; put in new floor mats (to keep remnants of the snowy Minnesota winters off the cabin carpeting)

***ELECTRONICS:*** installed a new stereo system to blast some of my favorite songs while working on homework in the Teg or cruising down the highway; added a fuzz buster (this awesome tool lets me know if a cop is using a radar gun to monitor my speed)